THE CURIOUS QUEST FOR
THE SANDMAN'S SAND

First performed at the Yvonne Arnaud Theatre, Guildford
on 19th June 1997 by the Yvonne Arnaud Youth Theatre
ACT 2, with the following cast:

Adult Actors

Harry, the Sandman	Simon Foster
Jewels, the Witch	Zoe Maddison

Act 2 Youth Theatre

Shiva Abassi-Ghadi	Olivia Oldroyd
Lucy Barwell	Edward Parry-Jones
Philip Bishop	Sam Phillips
Ben Browning	Stuart Saxon
James Cameron	Tara Scholes
Vita Cameron	Laura Seymour
Polly Cheal	Jonathan Slater
Alice Cook	Emma Stevens
Susannah Cook	Kit Stokes
Rebecca Dale	Abigail Thorncroft
Eleanore Duggan	Katie Thorncroft
James Martin	Hannah Turner
Katie McCalden	Matthew Veira
Lara Moss	Jo Whiteman

(The Yvonne Arnaud Youth Theatre ACT 2 comprises
local children aged between 7 and 13)

Production Team
Directed by Julia Burgess
Musical Director David Perkins
Lighting Design by John Harris

TEACHER'S NOTES

CHARACTER BREAKDOWN

The show can be adapted according to how many children you wish to have in the cast. The chorus roles can be played either by one group, or split into year groups for different scenes, thus allowing more children to take part.

MAIN PARTS

Harry the Sandman

Silver-tongued, zoot-suited deliverer of dreams with a cool jive-talking style. He needs to be a strong singer. This character acts as narrator and ought to be easily distinguishable from the rest of the company, which can be achieved by using either a teacher or an older student for the role.

SONGS: The Bed Bug Bop, The Sand Jive, Stealing the Sand (Gospel Prayer), Window Box Hill, The Sandman's Lullaby

Jewels the Witch

Beautiful and glamorous, but lacking any real skill in witchcraft, the part requires a brassy style and a powerful voice. A substantial role perhaps best played by a teacher or an older child.

SONGS: Jewels, The Spell, The Itch Calypso

Jesse

The eldest sibling. She is a responsible and sometimes bossy girl.

Meggie

The middle child, feisty and determined.

Teddy

Curious, sceptical, and little. And always hungry.

For visual humour, differences in height between the siblings can be emphasized. They must be strong speakers and confident with dialogue.

SONGS: The Bed Bug Bop, The Sand Jive, The Itch Calypso

Henchmen (1–4 suggested)

A comedy duo, though the Henchmen may be played by as many as four, and even as a solo.

SONGS: Jewels (they can also sing the chorus part in The Itch Calypso if required)

The Curious Quest For The Sandman's Sand

A musical

Book and Lyrics by Jenifer Toksvig
Music by David Perkins

Samuel French — London
New York - Toronto - Hollywood

Crumblitious
Kind, caring, and magical, the elderly Monk-Gardener of Window Box Hill
has a large speaking and singing part and could be played by a teacher or an
older child.
SONGS: The Pippitfly

Pippitfly
The Pippitfly should be cute, perhaps a younger child who is a good dancer
and can flutter her eyelashes at the audience appealingly.
SONGS: (None)

Trash Trump
An American GI, gruff yet friendly. He needs to have a loud voice and a good
sense of rhythm for his song.
SONGS: Trash Trump Dump

Gump Grump
A small character role requiring a loud speaking voice and, most importantly,
height no greater than Teddy's.
SONGS: (None)

CHORUS ROLES
BED BUG BOP:
Friends of Jesse, Meggie and Teddy (any number)
The opening song. It can be used to introduce the entire company, or to
provide an ensemble number for a group of any size and age.

STEALING THE SAND (GOSPEL PRAYER):
Gospel Choir (any number)
A Gospel Choir. They should be encouraged to be as expressive as possible.

TAPESTRY FAYRE:
The Train/Fairground attractions and crowd (any number)
The Fayre is a magical setting where the entire company can perform. It is
also, however, the ideal opportunity to provide smaller speaking and singing
roles for more confident members of the ensemble. For example, the Clowns
could be an acrobatic feature and the Daisytattle solo a ballet.
Attractions:
Clowns
Daisytattle(s) selling Cotton Pear (similar to Candy Floss)
The Fly 'n' Go Round. This is a carousel with "real" animals called Snoodle
Werps who fly around the central pole. The Snoodle Werps are ridden by the
children, so they could be props similar to hobby horses, or played by bigger

children in costume who can give piggy-back rides to Jessie, Meggie and Teddy. There is a Snoodle Barker, who attracts people to the ride, and it may be necessary to have children playing Snoodle Grooms, to hold the Snoodle Werps until the ride begins.

The Groogly Hog: train driver

Crowd:
As the land is populated by creatures, the "crowd" chorus can be made up either of children without special costume, or Scrumble Bees. These creatures have no particular purpose other than to add a splash of bright colour to the crowd, and to distinguish the three main children from the rest of the creatures.

THE SPELL, THE ITCH CALYPSO:
Hagglets and Habituals (any number)
These creatures are the perfect role for younger children who will enjoy the chance to make ugly faces. The group can be as large as required.

WINDOW BOX HILL, THE PIPPITFLY:
Monks (any number)
They help Crumblitious to tend Window Box Hill, and should be able to hold a simple line of harmony.
Villagers (any number)
An optional role in "Window Box Hill" for non-singing members of the ensemble.

TRASH TRUMP DUMP:
Litter Bugs (any number)
A role for children who can sing and march in time.

PROPERTIES
Suggested properties are given on page 37. However, these can be as simple or elaborate as resources allow.

COSTUME
It is easiest to use a basic costume, such as a particular colour T-shirt and shorts, and add accessories to identify each character. There are suggestions indicated on page 39. However, these can be simplified according to the available resources.

SET

All the action occurs within the children's bedroom. It is a bedroom, however, extended by their imagination to include each of the places they visit. For example, Window Box Hill is a magical garden that grows from the flowers in the window box outside, and Tapestry Fayre is a carnival that springs from the toy carousel that sits atop the toy box.

The bed provides a raised platform upon which certain scenes can take place. The set need not be complicated: large alphabet blocks can be used to create a variety of different locations, simply by painting appropriate images or letters on the sides.

The following is a suggestion for setting:

Basic Set:

Large rostra, centre stage, window frame hanging above the upstage end of the rostra; a large toy box; large alphabet blocks; a moon and stars mobile hanging to one side at the back of the set.

The Bedroom

The rostra can be made into a bed by placing a headboard at the upstage edge and using a simple sheet and three pillows.

The Train

The engine can be made with alphabet blocks, and the chorus can use small umbrellas for the wheels.

Tapestry Fayre

The umbrellas become the Fly 'n' Go Round on top of the bed, perhaps using a few alphabet blocks on the rostra to give an idea of height.

Jewels' Castle

The alphabet blocks can be used as a cauldron, or to build a castle wall.

Window Sill Falls

Blue fabric or paper, fastened to the bottom of the window frame and draped down over the front of the rostra, can be used for the water.

Window Box Hill

Alphabet blocks can be used to build trees and bushes.

Trash Trump Dump

The Litter Bugs appear at first to be the pile of rubbish. A sign can be used to indicate location.

Edgy Forest

One large, gnarled tree can be built from the alphabet blocks. The back of the Trash Trump Dump sign can indicate location.

Scene Changes

The show will run more smoothly if scene changes can be as short and simple as possible. To achieve this, it may help to use Harry's dialogue (with or without scene change music as underscoring) as a cover for each change of scene. A map of the journey can be used by Harry to indicated the location of each scene.

With thanks to Julia Burgess for the preparation of the Teacher's Notes.

COMPOSER'S NOTES

The Curious Quest for the Sandman's Sand is best performed with a full band of four musicians: piano, bass, drums/percussion, and tenor sax/Bb clarinet. It is possible to perform the show with a piano and drums, or even a piano alone. It should be noted, however, that several sections of the score are rhythm only. Scene change music can be used as underscoring for Harry's dialogue, either during or after the scene changes, if required. The piano score is available for hire, and should be used in rehearsals. The band parts are also available for hire.

MUSICAL NUMBERS

No. 1	**The Bed Bug Bop**	Harry, Jesse, Meggie, Teddy, Chorus
No. 2	**The Sand Jive**	Harry, Jesse, Meggie, Teddy
No. 3	**Stealing the Sand (Gospel Prayer)**	Harry, Jesse, Meggie, Teddy, Chorus
No. 3a	Exit Music	
No. 3b	Gump Grump (Sting)	
No. 3c	Gump Grump (Sting)	
No. 4	**Tapestry Fayre**	Ensemble
No. 4a	Scene Change Music/Underscoring (optional)	
No. 4b	Gump Grump (Sting)	
No. 4c	Spell and Crash Music	
No. 5	**Jewels**	Jewels, Henchmen
No. 5a	Gump Grump (Sting)	
No. 6	**The Spell**	Jewels, Chorus
No. 7	**The Itch Calypso**	Jesse, Meggie, Teddy, Jewels, Chorus
No. 7a	Gump Grump (Sting)	
No. 7b	Scene Change Music (optional)	
No. 8	**Window Box Hill**	Harry, Monks
No. 8a	Gump Grump (Sting)	
No. 9	**The Pippitfly**	Crumblitious, Monks
No. 9a	Scene Change Music (optional)	
No. 9b	Gump Grump (Sting)	
No. 9c	Gump Grump (Sting)	
No. 10	**The Trash Trump Dump**	Trash Trump, Litterbugs
No. 10a	Exit Music, Underscoring and Entrance of Gump Grump	
No. 11	The Final Conflict (instrumental underscore)	
No. 12	**The Sandman's Lullaby**	Harry
No. 13	**Finale (Reprise: Gospel Prayer)**	Ensemble
No. 13a	Bows	
No. 13b	**Encore (Reprise: The Bed Bug Bop)**	Ensemble
No. 13c	Exit Music	

The vocal score and band parts are available on hire from Samuel French Ltd.

For Jesse, Meggie, Teddy, Alex and Laura,
Katie, Libby and Ned.

THE CURIOUS QUEST FOR THE SANDMAN'S SAND

A children's bedroom. It is bedtime

The Narrator (Harry) is standing separately from the scene. Jesse, Meggie and Teddy are in the bed, and their friends, the chorus, are all around them. No-one in the town can sleep …

No. 1 The Bed Bug Bop

Harry	I've got a little story that I'd like to tell
	About some friends of mine who weren't sleeping well
	They couldn't get to sleep no matter how they tried
	They tossed, turned, and then they cried,
All	We've got the Bed Bug Bop
	We've got the Bed Bug Bop
	We've got the Bed Bug Bop
	We've got the Bed Bug Bop
	We're hopping and bopping and we just can't stop
	We've got the Bed Bug Bop
	We've got the Bed Bug Bop
Harry	Now Jessica Grace had had her fun
	And she was tuckered out because the day was done
Jesse	I wanna sleep but I don't think I can
Harry	And then she cried,
Jesse	You better believe it, man
	I've got the Bed Bug Bop
Chorus	She's got the Bed Bug Bop
Jesse	I've got the Bed Bug Bop
Chorus	She's got the Bed Bug Bop
Jesse	I've got the Bed Bug Bop
Chorus	She's got the Bed Bug Bop
Jesse	I've got the Bed Bug Bop
Chorus	She's got the Bed Bug, the Bed Bug Bop
Jesse	I'm hopping and bopping and I just can't stop

Jessie } (*together*) { I've got the Bed Bug Bop.
Chorus }   { She's got the Bed Bug Bop.

Harry   Now Megan Al had played away
                          She'd sung and swung all through the day
                          But instead of tired she felt alive,
Meggie   I wanna sleep but I gotta jive

                          I've got the Bed Bug Bop
Chorus   She's got the Bed Bug Bop
Meggie   I've got the Bed Bug Bop
Chorus   She's got the Bed Bug Bop
Meggie   I've got the Bed Bug Bop
Chorus   She's got the Bed Bug Bop
Meggie   I've got the Bed Bug Bop
Chorus   She's got the Bed Bug, the Bed Bug Bop
Meggie   I'm hopping and bopping and I just can't stop
                          I've got the Bed Bug Bop
Meggie } (*together*) { I've got the Bed Bug Bop.
Chorus }   { She's got the Bed Bug Bop.

Harry   Theodore Luke is this boy's name
                          Teddy to his friends, if it's all the same
                          And sleeping is his favourite game
Harry   But now he said,
Teddy   It's a crying shame

                          I've got the Bed Bug Bop
Chorus   He's got the Bed Bug Bop
Teddy   I've got the Bed Bug Bop
Chorus   He's got the Bed Bug Bop
Teddy   I've got the Bed Bug Bop
Chorus   He's got the Bed Bug Bop
Teddy   I've got the Bed Bug Bop
Chorus   He's got the Bed Bug, the Bed Bug Bop
Teddy   I'm hopping and bopping and I just can't stop
                          I've got the Bed Bug Bop
Teddy } (*together*) { I've got the Bed Bug Bop.
Chorus }   { He's got the Bed Bug Bop.

Optional dance break

Harry	And all their friends around the town
	Were trying to make their feet slow down
All	We're jumpy, grumpy, got the itch
	We're trying to slow down but our feet just twitch

Chorus 1	We've got the Bed Bug Bop
Chorus 2	We've got the Bed Bug Bop
Chorus 1	We've got the Bed Bug Bop
Chorus 2	We've got the Bed Bug Bop
Chorus 1	We've got the Bed Bug Bop
Chorus 2	We've got the Bed Bug Bop

Chorus 1	We've got the Bed Bug Bop
Chorus 2	We've got the Bed Bug, the Bed Bug Bop
Chorus	We're hopping and bopping and we just can't stop
	We've got the Bed Bug Bop
	We've got the Bed Bug Bop

All	We're hopping, bopping,
	Jiving and diving,
	Mopping, popping,
	Hiving and thriving.
	We're scooting, squealing,
	Hooting and reeling,
	Peaking, poking,
	Squeaking and joking.
	We're swaying, playing,
	Feeling in the pink.
	Don't think we'll ever stop
	With the Bed Bug, with the Bed Bug,
	With the Bed Bug, with the Bed Bug Bop
	With the Bed Bug Bop.

Harry and the other children exit, leaving Jesse, Meggie and Teddy

Lighting change. The three children are watching the town from their bedroom window. A distant clock strikes midnight under the dialogue

Meggie Jesse, look ... all the lights are on, all over the town.
Jesse I know ... looks like we're not the only ones who can't sleep, Meg. I wonder why? Something must have happened.
Teddy Something like what, Jess?
Jesse If I knew that, Teddy, I wouldn't be asking, would I?

Teddy Well, I am going to *try* and go to sleep, because I am only little and if I *don't* sleep, I'll get grumpy.

All three children lie down as if to go to sleep

Harry appears quietly from behind the bed, and peers down at the children over the bedhead

Teddy is the only one who notices him at first

Teddy Er, Jesse …
Jesse I thought you were going to sleep, Teddy?
Teddy I can't, and now there's a man looking at me …
Meggie Where? What man?
Teddy Umm … that one, there … leaning over the headboard.
Meggie (*hiding underneath a pillow*) Does he look scary?
Teddy Umm … no, I don't think he's scary. In fact, he doesn't even look very … real.
Harry Real?

Harry walks around to the side of the bed, and Jesse, Meggie and Teddy huddle together a little

No: 2 The Sand Jive

Dialogue underscored until top of song

Harry I am 'bout as *real* as they come, my little friend. I am the keeper and distributor of the stuff that dreams are made of. I am the Main Man, the Head Honcho, the Big Cheese, the Be All and End All of Righteous Reverie. I (*pause for effect*) am the Sandman. Who — are *you*?
Jesse Umm, I'm Jesse.
Harry (*raising his hat*) Delighted, little sister.
Teddy She's *my* sister, and so is she, and she's Meggie, and I'm Teddy, and I'm only little … pleased to meet you.
Meggie Do *you* have a name?

Harry walks forwards into the light. All three children stare at the man

Harry (*speaking*)   I'm Harensabule Tofustus Virago the Fourth.
Jesse
Meggie } (*speaking Who?
Teddy   together*)

Harry (*speaking*)   Harensabule Tofustus Virago the Fourth.

Jesse
Meggie } (*speaking together*)   Who?
Teddy

Harry (*speaking*)   Harensabule Tofustus Virago the Fourth.
                          But you can call me Harry for short.

Jesse
Meggie } (*speaking together*)   Oh.
Teddy

Musical interlude as the kids ponder this fact

                          Hang on. Where did you come from?
Harry (*singing*)   Well I ask you, what kind of a question is that?
                          Now can't you tell by the tilt of my hat?
                          It's a place that ain't quite anywhere
                          It's a place that ain't quite there

Jesse
Meggie } (*speaking together*)   Where?
Teddy

Harry   I come from the place where they dole out the dream
                          The spot where it's hot not to be as you seem
                          Be awake, as it were, with your eyes shut tight
                          The place that hangs out at the edge of the night.

                          Now can't you tell I'm a dude with a new attitude
                          Wa-wa-wa!
                          This ain't no boast, and I'm not try'n' to be rude.
                          The friends I keep call me Mister Sleep
                          There ain't no fuss, I just take some dust
                          And spread that sand all over the land
                          It gets in your eyes and a Big Surprise!
                          It's rock-a-bye time, rock-a-bye time, rock-a-bye
                            time,
                          That ain't no crime.

                          You go shake, shake, rock the land
                          Gotta take that sand in the palm of your hand
                          And go shake, shake, rock the land
                          Let's give it on up for that sleeping sand.

                          Gotta shake it, make it time to kip
                          Do it with me, guys, it's just a pip

               This ain't no drink that you gotta sip
               Gonna shake it on out, shake it on out, it's just too hip.

All   You go shake, shake, rock the land
               Gotta take that sand in the palm of your hand
               And go shake, shake rock the land
               Let's give it on up for that sleeping sand.

(*Speaking*)   You go shake, shake, rock the land
               Gotta take that sand in the palm of your hand
               And go shake, shake, rock the land
(*Singing*)   Let's give it on up, give it on up, give it on up.
(*Speaking*)   Give it on up!
(*Singing*)   For that sleeping sand
Jesse   For that sleeping sand
Meggie   For that sleeping sand
Teddy   For that sleeping sand
Harry   For that sleeping …
All (*whispering*) *Sand!*

Jesse So let me get this straight, Harry — you send everyone to sleep by sprinkling sand over them, right?

Harry That is affirmative, Little Sister.

Meggie So how come we're not sleeping, Mr I'm So Clever?

Jesse
Meggie } (*together*) Yeah — where's the sand?
Teddy

Harry I am embarrassed to tell you my tale of woe. You see, my sleepin' sand has temporarily strayed from my possession. Matter-of-factly, it has been expropriated without my given consent.

During this long and boring speech, Teddy nods off. Meggie notices this

Meggie Hey! You made Teddy go to sleep!

Jesse (*looking at Teddy*) No, I think you just bored him with all those long words. (*She pushes Teddy*)

Teddy (*waking up*) Hmm? Oh, what were you saying about the sand?

Harry Somebody stole it.

Jesse Somebody stole your sand? Who?

Harry Ah, the story, my friends, is a sad one. (*He snaps his fingers*)

A Gospel Choir enters in a heavenly light

Teddy Who are *they*?

Harry Ladies and gentlemen, may I introduce Harry's Heavenly Host. Don't you know 'em? Why they sing you to sleep every night …

Teddy (*mumbling*) Never happened to me … I've never seen a Heavenly Wotsit …

Harry Please … a little respect. (*He clears his throat*) Now, it all happened like this …

During this song, the actions of the Crovel can be mimed by a member of the choir

No: 3 Stealing the Sand (Gospel Prayer)

| (*Singing*) | The Sand … |
| **Chorus** | Oh, the Sand |

Teddy (*whispering to Jesse and Meggie*) I think he's going to sing about the Sand.

Harry (*speaking*) Shh!

| (*Singing*) | The Sand … |
| **Chorus** | Oh, the Sand |

Teddy (*whispering to Jesse and Meggie*) See? I told you so.

Harry (*speaking*) Shh!

| (*Singing*) | Just the other day, my friends |
| **Chorus** | The other day Yay Yay Yay |

Harry (*speaking*) Will you guys shut up! You're cramping my style.

Chorus Sorry, Harry, yeah, sorry. We're just doing our job.

Harry (*singing*)	The other day, I was walking along, humming my song
Chorus	Mm-mm …
Harry	Just waiting, waiting for night to fall
Chorus	That's all …
Harry	When I heard a crying sound, a–echoing around the hall.
Chorus	Around the hall
Harry	So I went to check it out, like any good Boy Scout would do,
	Like any good Boy Scout would do.

Chorus	Do be do do
Harry	And guess what I found?
Chorus	What?
Harry	A-lyin' on the ground?
Chrous	What?
Harry	I found a Crovel.
Chorus	Who?
Harry	I found a Crovel.
Chorus	Ooo ...

Teddy (*speaking*) Wait a minute, wait a minute! Crovel?

Harry Yeah, Crovel ... you know, creature with legs, arms, likes to crovel ... Hmm ... Professor!

Professor, a member of the Gospel Choir, steps forwards

Professor The Cadeo Adularius, or Crovel, is a small animal of uncertain origin, with crinkly skin and many arms and legs. These appendages make walking very difficult for it, and consequently it spends much of its time on the floor, having fallen over itself. It has come to be known as a Crovel, because of its tendency to crovel. Thank you.

Harry (*to Teddy*) OK?

Teddy Oh yes, it's all very clear now, thank you. Crovel ... should have known ...

Harry And he was just lyin' there, the poor little creature, miles away from home (sob) cryin' to himself, just lyin' there cryin', and sighin' and cryin' and lyin' and sighin' ...

Chorus OK, we get the idea. Then what happened?

Harry So I put down my bag of sand, and I went up to that poor little thing and I said, "Now hey, little fella, what you cryin' fer? Did somebody do something to hurt you?"

Chorus Oh ...

Harry And you know what he said?

Chorus No ...

Harry   He said,

(*Singing*)   "Nobody hurt me, you great big heel,
                      But you got something I wanna steal.
                      I got this itch that I gotta scratch, see?
                      Chase me if you want but you'll never catch me.
                      The Gump Grump ordered a bag of sand

> He's big and bad and he's in command.
> So I'll take that sand and be off at the double.
> Don't try and follow, or there'll be big trouble!"

Teddy (*speaking*) Wait a minute, wait a minute! What?

Professor steps forward again

Professor Allow me to explain. You see, the Crovel works for the Gump
Grump ——
Teddy Of course he does …
Professor — who never sleeps and is therefore always grumpy. He sent the
Crovel to steal Harry's sand, thereby ensuring that no-one can sleep. He
believes that if he is grumpy, everyone else should be grumpy too. Is that
clear?

Jessie
Meggie } (*together*) Oh … you mean … He said,
Teddy

(*Singing*)   "Nobody hurt me, you great big heel,
        But you got something I wanna steal.
        I got this itch that I gotta scratch, see?
        Chase me if you want but you'll never catch me.
        The Gump Grump ordered a bag of sand
        He's big and bad and he's in command.
        So I'll take that sand and be off at the double.
        Don't try and follow, or there'll be big trouble!"
Chorus   Oo, there'll be big trouble.
        Oo, there'll be big trouble.
        Oo, big trouble. Oo, big trouble.

Teddy (*speaking*) Why didn't you say that in the first place?

Harry (*speaking*)   I went to grab the bag but, unfortunately, he had a head
        start.
        He was smart and my heart is torn apart. You gotta …
        Help me!
Chorus (*singing*)   Help him!
Harry (*speaking*)   Help me …
Chorus (*singing*)   Help him!
Harry (*speaking*)   Help me …

Chorus (*singing*)	Help him!
Harry (*speaking*)	Help me …
Chorus (*singing*)	Help him!
Harry (*speaking*)	Help me …
Chorus (*singing*)	Help him!
Harry (*speaking*)	Help me …
Chorus (*singing*)	Help him!

Harry (*speaking*) *Stop!*

	You gotta help me (*singing*) find the sand, yeh yeh yeh yeh yeh!
	So I can spread my glorious sleep all over the land.
Chorus	Yeh yeh yeh yeh!
All	Amen!

Music stops as if it is the end of the song

Harry (*speaking*) So, how about it? Are you guys gonna help me out here?

All (*singing*)   Oh, yeah!

No. 3a – Exit Music

The Gospel Choir make a swift exit

The three children are alone with Harry

Jesse Come on, Harry! Let's go and get your sleeping sand back from the Gump Grump!

No. 3b – Gump Grump (sting)

Teddy What was that?
Harry (*looking around furtively*) Shh! Don't say that name too loud …
Meggie What, Gump Grump?

No. 3c – Gump Grump (sting)

Harry Well, I'll let you get going. Thank you, thank you, and thank you. Good luck!

Harry walks away as if business is done

Teddy Hang on … how are we going to get there?

Harry Ah! What you need is an excess of express. I mean, you can just take the train.

Jessie
Meggie } (*together*) What train?
Teddy

Harry picks up a toy train and rolls it off stage

Lighting change

A large train comes on, with the Fairground Chorus using umbrellas to make the wheels of the carriages. The Groogly Hog is driving the train

The three children take flags from the toy box and join the train. During this song, they are "taken" to Tapestry Fayre as the scene is changed around them. The children making up the train become fairground attractions/ crowd: Clowns, Daisytattle(s), Snoodle Barker and Grooms, etc. The umbrellas can be used to make the Fly 'n' Go Round canopy

No. 4 Tapestry Fayre

Chorus (*chanting*)   Tapestry Fayre, Tapestry Fayre,
                             Everyone from everywhere
                             Loves to see the jamboree
                             At Tapestry, Tapestry Fayre!

                             Tapestry Fayre, Tapestry Fayre,
                             Everyone from everywhere
                             Loves to see the jamboree
                             At Tapestry, Tapestry Fayre!

Harry Take it easy now! It could be dangerous!

Chorus 1	Tapestry Fayre, Tapestry Fayre …
Chorus 2	Tapestry Fayre, Tapestry Fayre …
Chorus 1	Everyone from everywhere …
Chorus 2	Everyone from everywhere …
Chorus 1	Loves to see the jamboree …
Chorus 2	Loves to see the jamboree …
Chorus 1	At Tapestry, Tapestry Fayre!
Chorus 2	At Tapestry, Tapestry Fayre!

Chorus 1

Tapestry Fayre, Tapestry Fayre
Everyone from everywhere
Loves to see the jamboree
At Tapestry, Tapestry Fayre!
Tapestry Fayre, Tapestry Fayre
Everyone from everywhere
Loves to see the jamboree
At Tapestry, Tapestry Fayre!

Chorus 2

Tapestry Fayre, Tapestry Fayre
Everyone from everywhere
Loves to see the jamboree
At Tapestry, Tapestry Fayre!
Tapestry Fayre, Tapestry Fayre
Everyone from everywhere
Loves to see the Fayre!

Groogly Hog Tapestry Fayre! Tapestry Fayre! This stop Tapestry Fayre!

Jesse Look, Teddy! Clowns!

The Clowns dance and pretend to throw water over each other, using buckets containing glitter

Then Daisytattle(s) appear, with "candy-floss" on sticks: it is Cotton Pear

Daisytattle(s)   Cotton Pear! Cotton Pear!
Come and get your lovely Cotton Pear!
Everything's free at Tapestry Fayre! Cotton Pear!

Teddy Can we have some, Jesse? I'm starving.

The Daisytattle(s) do a little dance with their Cotton Pear. As they give it to the crowd around them, Jesse, Meggie and Teddy have to wait until last to be served. When they get there, it has all gone

Daisytattle(s) I am sorry, children. There isn't any more.
Teddy But I'm starving! If I don't eat soon, I'll be too tired to walk much further!
Snoodle Barker Don't worry about that, my friend. Climb on a Snoodle Werp to rest your weary legs. They'll fly you as high as you want to go. There ain't no walking involved.

The Fly n'Go Round is similar to a Carousel, except that the animals on the side are all Snoodle Werps. They are not attached to the ride, but are "live" creatures who fly around and around the central pole. (See the Teacher's Notes on page v)

Meggie A Snoodle Werp?
Teddy (*sighing*) Here we go again.

Jesse Well, obviously, that is a Snoodle Werp. You know — big, pink thing with … well … wings … and … stuff. You know, Snoodle Werp.

Teddy pinches Meggie

Meggie Ow! Teddy! Why did you pinch me?
Teddy I wanted to be absolutely certain that we were all awake.

The children each climb aboard a Snoodle Werp and the ride begins to go round. As they fly around, the music builds and they seem to climb higher and higher above the Fayre, and eventually fly out over the surrounding land

The people at the Fayre slowly exit backwards, as if they are receding into the distance

Jessie, Meggie and Teddy look out over the audience, giving the impression they are very high up

Jesse Yippee!
Meggie This is brilliant!
Teddy This is *high*!
Meggie Look how small the Fayre is getting!
Teddy (*trying not to look*) I am, I am …
Jesse Everything is so tiny. Look! There's a castle over there! Let's fly over that!

Jessie, Meggie and Teddy exit

No. 4a Scene Change Music/Underscoring (optional)

The focus switches to Harry, in his spotlight away from the action on stage. During Harry's dialogue, the scene is changed to the castle of Jewels the Witch

Harry No, no, no. That ain't the right way to go! That's where Jewels the Witch lives, and when you walk into that old witch-woman, you are walking right into Trouble with a capital T. That washed-out ol' hag, she ain't good for nothing 'cept bad spells and dirty smells, I'm tellin' ya. Why, I remember one time she turned her own mother into a big, fat, hairy, greasy toad. Or maybe her mother already was a big, fat, hairy, greasy toad … I wish I could have gone with them kids, but what with my bad leg and all, not to mention … well, maybe I shouldn't mention it. Anyhow, let's go see what Jewels the Witch is gonna do to them now that they're on her turf. This ain't looking good. It ain't looking good at *all*. I sure hope they don't tell her about the Gump Grump …

Lighting change

No. 4b Gump Grump (sting)

Jewels enters with her Henchmen and looks off stage to see the children flying overhead

Jewels Children! And Snoodle Werps! My favourite combination … (*She laughs maniacally*)

No. 4c Spell and Crash Music

Jewels casts a spell at the children, accompanied by much thunder and lightning

Jessie, Meggie and Teddy enter slightly dazed, as if they have crash-landed

Teddy My Snoodle Werp crashed! (*After a pause to think about this*) What am I saying?
Jewels Mmmm … I have such a *thing* for Crashed Snoodle Werp Stew …

No. 5 Jewels

(*Singing*)	There are things I have a thing for
	Some are silver, some are gold.
	There are things I have a thing for,
	Some are new and some are very old.
	But the thing I have a thing for most
	And to that thing I raise a toast is
	Being a witch, it
(*Speaking*)	Gives me an itch,
	Let me (*singing*) introduce your host …
(*Speaking*)	I'm Jewels …
Henchmen	We call her Jewels
Jewels (*speaking*)	I make the rules
Henchmen	She makes the rules
Jewels (*speaking*)	If it's a spell you need
	With just a pinch of greed
(*Singing*)	And a few entrails
	That's all it entails,
(*Speaking*)	I'll bake ...
Henchmen	You bet she'll bake
Jewels (*speaking*)	I'll make a cake ...

Henchmen   She'll make a cake
Jewels (*speaking*)   I'll add to a stew
                          A rat's tail or two.
(*Singing*)   Some ripened toad
                          A flattened fox from the road
                          And then ... (*Two finger clicks*)

Henchmen (*speaking*) She'll have to start again.
Jewels (*speaking*) Shut up, you revolting little vermin!

(*Singing*)   I may not be the best, you see,
                          But I have had successes.
                          There've been some mishaps, I agree
                          Especially with princesses.
Henchmen   Her only poisoned apple was
                          The best that she could make.
                          That princess ate the whole thing up
                          And then she didn't even get a stomach ache.
Jewels (*more spoken than sung*)
                          I tried to build a hedge of thorns
                          And a cottage made of sweets.
                          I wanted something prickly
                          And some yummy, scrummy treats.
Henchmen   Instead of thorns she conjured up
                          A load of fruit and veg.
                          The cottage tasted horrible
                          And the prince just ate the hedge.

Jewels (*speaking*) I'm bad ...

Henchmen   She's very bad!

Jewels (*speaking*) No, I mean *bad*!

Henchmen (*speaking*) She's *really bad*!
Jewels   I don't play by the rules
                           I don't go to no schools
                           For my spell-making tools.

(*A sigh; speaking*) I'm surrounded by fools ...

Jewels   } (*singing   { I'm Jewels!
Henchmen   } together*)   { She's Jewels!

Jewels (*to the Henchmen*) Fetch my Hagglets and Habituals!

The Henchmen exit and return with the Hagglets and Habituals during the following

(*To the children*) *You* invaded *my* air space. Might I enquire as to your purpose here?

Jesse Um … well …

Meggie You see, the Sandman's Magic Sand ——

Teddy (*whispering*) Meggie! Don't tell her! She's a witch!

Jesse — has been stolen by the Gump Grump ——

Teddy (*whispering*) Jesse, I really think this is a bad idea …

Meggie — and now no-one can sleep ——

Jesse — so we've got to find him and get it back ——

Meggie — so that we can all go to sleep again.

Teddy (*whispering and making signals to Jesse and Meggie*) No! No! Witch! Witch!

Jesse So we were wondering if you could possibly ——

Jewels My darlings, but how sweet of you to come to me! I'm always keen to lend a hand to those in need …

Henchmen Yeah, those in need of being turned into a toad! Heh heh heh.

Jewels Come here, you blithering idiots … (*Aside to the Henchmen and the audience*) This sand must be pretty powerful if that nasty creature wants it so badly. Hmm … I feel a spell coming on …

Henchman 1 Oh no … we've only just got back to normal after the *last* spell …

Henchman 2 Yeah, but having two heads each meant we could *eat* more …

Jewels Silence! Now, there has to be a way to get the sand from that vile creature, the Gump Grump.

No. 5a Gump Grump (sting)

I've got it! I will give the children a present to take him … I'll make a potion that will make him itch, and twitch. We'll follow the children to his lair in Edgy Forest, and when they give him the potion, he'll start to itch and *drop* the sand. Then we can grab it while he isn't looking. Hah! I love days like this, when everything just seems to go right for me.

Henchman Don't hold your breath, will you …

Jewels (*to the children*) Children, this is your very lucky day. I am going to give you a present for the Gump Grump. It will make him so happy, that he will give you the sand without a second thought.

Henchmen (*aside to each other*) It'll end in tears …

Jesse Oh, thank you.

Meggie We'd be ever so grateful.
Teddy I *really* think this is a bad idea ...

Some or all of the items mentioned in the following song can be produced and used or mimed. One of the alphabet blocks can be turned upside down for a cauldron, or a separate one painted as such

No. 6 The Spell

Jewels (*singing*)	A spell!
	A spell!
(*Speaking*)	Come to me, my beautiful Book of Incantation.
	Together we'll make a dream full of wild imagination,
	A spell that will run its fingers through your hair
	And close the eyes of children everywhere.
Chorus (*singing*)	A spell!
	A spell!
Jewels	Fetch me the cauldron, round and black as night.
Chorus	The fire beneath is heating fast.
Jewels	Fill it with icy drops of pale moonlight.
Chorus	The drums of night go beating past.
Jewels	A living snake in twisted coil
	Will make our sordid mixture boil.
Chorus	The witching hour of midnight's here at last.
Jewels	Fetch me a jar of bat wings soaked in spice.
Chorus	The smoke is climbing to the sky
Jewels	The skin of a toad, the tails of two young mice
Chorus	A mist upon the ground will lie
Jewels	A pinch of skin from one small child
	The night will be bewitched, beguiled
Chorus	The world will be in darkness by and by
Jewels	A spell!
	A spell!
(*Speaking*)	A drop of blood will shade it with the deepest red
	A lock of yellow hair plucked from the youngest head
	The brown earth of a grave that's freshly dug
	The comfort of a Boa Constrictor's hug
Chorus (*singing*)	A spell ...
	A spell
Jewels	I summon up the spirits of the night
Chorus	The beating drum will hypnotize
Jewels	To hear my call and step into the light
Chorus	The wind is roaring through the skies

Jewels	Breathe life into my potion and
	Obey me now, as I command
Chorus	We see the spirits as they rise …

The music pauses. She waves a wand over the cauldron as she chants to the spirits

Jewels (*chanting*)	*Cum fluxia ite, pueri!*
Henchmen	What?
Jewels (*aside*)	Go with the flow, boys.

The music builds into a crescendo as Jewels fills a goblet with potion (talcum powder) and walks towards the children. She trips accidentally, and potion is spilt over Jesse, Meggie and Teddy. There is a momentary pause, during which we see that Jewels is obviously furious that this has happened

Argh! You clumsy fools! Look what you've made me do!

Slowly, the three children begin to itch. During the opening of the next number, Jewels' expression changes to one of utter joy that she has finally created a potion that actually does what it is supposed to. The Henchmen register obvious shock at this. The music segues into:

No. 7 The Itch Calypso

The following is spoken

Jesse	
Meggie }	Hey!
Teddy	
Jewels	Can this be real?
Jesse	
Meggie }	You witch!
Teddy	
Jewels	Can it be true?
Jesse	
Meggie }	My arms!
Teddy	
Jewels	How do they feel?
Jesse	
Meggie }	They itch!
Teddy	
Jewels	Just look at you!

| Jesse Meggie Teddy | That present You planned Won't get The sand. Itchy legs, Itchy face, In fact, we itch all over the place! |

Jewels It works! I created a spell that works! (*She trills a Calypso arriba*)

The lighting changes to a sunny Caribbean effect. The following is sung, during which the Henchmen can play maracas

Chorus Dey itch, dey itch, dey itch, see how dey twitch.
Dey itch, dey itch, dey itch see how dey twitch.

| Jesse Meggie Teddy | The potion that you made was not much good. It didn't work like a proper potion should. We wanted to sleep, but that will have to keep. We'd stop ourselves from itching if we could. |

Chorus Dey itch, dey itch, dey itch, see how dey twitch.
Dey itch, dey itch, dey itch, see how dey twitch.

| Jesse Meggie Teddy | The powder that you spilt has made us itch, And now we know the truth, you bad old witch. You fooled us all along, the ingredients were wrong, And now this itching powder's made us twitch. |

Chorus Dey itch, dey itch, dey itch, see how dey twitch.
Dey itch, dey itch, dey itch, see how dey twitch.

The following is spoken unless indicated otherwise

Jesse Meggie Teddy	My elbows...
Jewels	Scratch those elbows!
Jesse Meggie Teddy	My feet...
Jewels	Yeah, scratch those feet!
Jesse Meggie Teddy	My shoulders ...

Jewels		Scratch those shoulders, boy!
Jesse **Meggie** **Teddy**	}	My ears?!
Jewels		That bit's an extra treat!
Chorus (*singing*)		Dey itch …
Jewels		And ain't it good to see!
Chorus (*singing*)		Dey itch …
Jewels		Just how good can it be?
Chorus (*singing*)		Dey itch …
Jewels		That part's completely free!
Chorus (*singing*)		Dey itch …
Jessie **Meggie** **Teddy**	} (*singing*)	We need to find a tall banana tree So we can scratch these itches and be free. We'd dive into the ocean to wash off all the potion But in this land we cannot see the sea.
Chorus (*singing*)		Dey itch, dey itch, dey itch, see how dey twitch. Dey itch, dey itch, dey itch, see how they twitch.
Jesse **Meggie** **Teddy**	}	My tummy!
Jewels		Scratch your tummy!
Jesse **Meggie** **Teddy**	}	My knees!
Jewels		Yeah, scratch those knees!
Jesse **Meggie** **Teddy**	}	My fingers!
Jewels		Scratch those fingers, girl!
Jesse **Meggie** **Teddy**	}	My nose?!
Jewels		Look out! She's gonna sneeze!
Chorus (*singing*)		Dey itch …
Jewels		And ain't it good to see!
Chorus (*singing*)		Dey itch …
Jewels		Just how good can it be?
Chorus (*singing*)		Dey itch …
Jewels		That part's completely free!
Chorus (*singing*)		Dey itch … Dey itch …
Jewels		And ain't it good to see!

Chorus (*singing*)	Dey itch …
Jewels	Just how good can it be?
Chorus (*singing*)	Dey itch …
Jewels	That part's completely free!
Chorus (*singing*)	Dey itch …
	Dey itch …
Henchmen	We can't believe it!
Chorus (*singing*)	Dey itch …
Jewels	You better believe it boys!
Chorus (*singing*)	Dey itch …
Jewels	Mama's cooking now!
Jewels } (*singing* **Chorus** } *together*)	Dey itch!

The music builds to a big finish as Jewels, Henchmen and Hagglets and Habituals dance around, screaming and laughing whilst the children continue to itch

Teddy I have a question!

Jewels No time for that now, child — you must hurry to Edgy Forest with the present for the Gump Grump!

No. 7a Gump Grump (sting)

She fills the goblet from the cauldron again and gives it to Jesse

Teddy But this is *itching powder* …

Jewels (*looking terribly pleased with herself*) Yes, it is, isn't it.

Meggie So, the Gump Grump will *want* that, will he?

Jesse Yes, I thought you said it would be something nice.

Jewels (*floundering a little at first*) Well, of course … I mean … (*To the Henchmen*) Help me out here …

Henchman Itching powder is … umm …

Henchman … his favourite thing to eat!

Teddy (*rubbing his growling stomach*) Oh, now *that* I can understand …

Jewels Run along now, like good children … Edgy Forest awaits …

The children exit, still itching madly

Hah! My plan is working well already. Henchmen!

Henchmen Yes, Your Nastiness?

Jewels Follow them. No, follow me as I follow them … I mean, after them, no, I mean before them, after me … Oh, just *come on*!

Henchmen Umm ... right-o!
Jewels (*sighing*) Fools, everywhere ...

Jewels, the Henchmen and the Hagglets and Habituals exit after the children

No. 7b Scene Change Music (optional)

The lights fade to a spot on Harry. As he speaks, the scene is changed to Window Box Hill/Windowsill Falls

Harry Things are not looking good for those kids. Why, they must be feeling pretty tired by now, and they ain't no closer to finding my Sand. That old witch got 'em fooled, all right. Now they are taking that itching powder to the Gump Grump in Edgy Forest, and there's no telling what he'll do to 'em when he starts itchin'. Say, I don't think they even know where Edgy Forest *is* ... Let's see where they got to ...

Lighting change as the children enter and approach a beautiful waterfall. They are tired, hungry and still itching. The garden can be made while the children are talking at the waterfall

Jesse Right then ... Edgy Forest ...
Meggie Yes, off to Edgy Forest ...
Teddy Um, which is where, exactly?
Jesse Ah ...
Meggie Oh ...
Teddy Look, we don't know where Edgy Forest *is*, and I am tired, and hungry, and I itch. Couldn't we at least wash the itching powder off in this waterfall?
Jesse I suppose we could stop for a minute ...

Lighting change. They begin to wash the powder off in the waterfall. Meggie notices the garden that lies beyond it

Meggie Jesse, Teddy, look ... what a beautiful garden. Are those fruit trees?
Teddy Fruit? As in food?
Jesse It looks delicious. I bet you could get really good Fried Fluke Fritters there.
Teddy Fried what? No, don't bother explaining. If you can eat it, I don't care *what* it's called.

They wander into the garden. Teddy reaches up to take a piece of Oozeberry Pie from a tree

Meggie Teddy! Don't do that.
Teddy Why not? I'm starving.
Jesse But we haven't been invited, Teddy. I wonder whose garden it is anyway?

As the children continue to wander around and look at all the delicious food, Harry sings of the garden

> *During the introduction to the song, Crumblitious and the Monks enter, through the audience if desired. The Monks carry punnets and Crumblitious has a bag of magical seeds, and one of green pippit cheese. The contents of both can be mimed*

No. 8 Window Box Hill

Harry	Imagine the juiciest, ripest tomatoes, Red as a clown nose and fresh as the dawn. Picture an onion, sliced through the middle, Pungent, and white as a unicorn's horn.
	Where could you find them, these ripe juicy fruits?
Monks	Why, they're grown by Crumblitious on Window Box Hill.
Harry	Fruits more delicious than any you've tasted.
Monks	Food more delicious than any you will.
Harry	Here, through the softest brown furrows of earth He carries the small bag of seeds he must sow, And under the moonlight he scatters them gently …
Monks (*Speaking*)	… Gently, gently, gently, Then covers them up with his magical hoe.
Harry	A sprinkling of rainwater, drawn from the rooftop,
Monks 1	A dusting of moonbeams,
Monks 2	A wish and a prayer,
Harry	And then old Crumblitious must tend to the garden Of strange and unusual plants that are there.
	Apart from tomatoes, and onions, and mushrooms, And cabbages, melons, and peaches on trees, Crumblitious grows magical, mystical foods Like Marmalade Pottings and Green Pippit Cheese.
	There are bushes of Bubble Pears, covered with nets To capture the ripe ones that float to the skies,

Monks   And patches of Pickling Peas, yellow and bitter,
                       Next to a tree full of Oozeberry pies.

Optional dance break

*During this, Villagers can enter to get food from the garden. They carry
baskets for the food*

Harry   The greenest of orchards shades a thick carpet
                       Of fallen-down nuts you can crunch with your boots:
                       Hog Nuts and Dough Nuts and Spiky So-So Nuts,
                       Tumbling down on to Rag Tassle Roots.

                       Crumblitious's favourite is down in the corner;
                       A patch of green grass that seems empty and bare
                       Until a cool breeze brings the faintest aroma …
Monks   … 'oma, 'oma, 'oma,
All (*whispering*) … To say that invisible Myth Cheese grows there.
Harry (*singing*) So if you should hunger for Crunchy Cobcornal
                       Or inkle for Knuck Weed with Chuckleseed Dill,
                       Pick up a basket and visit Crumblitious
                       Out in the moonlight …
All   On Window Box Hill.

If the Villagers have entered, they now exit, waving goodbye to the Monks

Crumblitious Good-evening, children. Welcome to my garden. Are you
looking for something in particular?
Jesse Well actually, we are rather hungry.
Teddy Rather hungry?! I'm starving. I have to keep up my strength, you
know. I am only little.
Meggie Teddy, if you say that one more time, so help me, I'll ——
Crumblitious Children, children! Please, do not argue. The garden is a place
for peace and thoughtfulness, not for fighting.
Jesse I'm sorry, but we have been through quite a lot tonight. First of all this
strange man appeared in our bedroom …
Meggie And we couldn't sleep …
Teddy And then we went to the Fayre, which I liked a lot …
Jesse And what with all the itching powder and everything …
Teddy Not to mention the Gump Grump …

No. 8a Gump Grump (sting)

Crumblitious Well then, perhaps you had better eat something before your
journey continues …

Teddy reaches for a slice of pie again, but before he can get it, Crumblitious hears a noise off stage that indicates the presence of Jewels the Witch and her Henchmen hiding in the garden. His expression changes to one of fear, and he shuffles the children to one side. They do not notice the intruders

Henchman (*off*) Look! Bubble Pears! I love Bubble Pears!
Jewels (*off*) Shhh! Idiot! We don't want them to know we are here, do we?
Crumblitious Errr … unfortunately, it is probably best if you hurry along with your journey.
Teddy (*desperately pointing to the pie*) But …
Crumblitious Please children, it is not safe for you here …
Jesse But how do we get to Edgy Forest?
Meggie Can you take us there?
Crumblitious (*whispering*) I cannot, my child … I must stay and protect the garden. However, the Pippitfly will lead you there as fast as she can fly.

The Pippitfly enters. She has no wings

Meggie How can she fly? She hasn't got any wings …
Crumblitious Ah yes, well there is just one slightly unusual thing you need to know …
Teddy Oh really? Now that makes a change here …
Crumblitious Whenever you want her to fly, simply feed her a piece of this. (*He hands them a hessian bag containing cheese*)
Teddy (*sniffing in the bag*) It smells like cheese. Can we all have some? I am *starving* …
Meggie Teddy!

By the end of the number, the children have managed to slip out of the garden with the Pippitfly

No. 9 The Pippitfly

Crumblitious	Oh the Pippitfly flies
	In a strange and wondrous way.
Monks (*speaking*)	Yeah Sister!
Crumblitious	When the Pippitfly flies,
	Which she does most every day,
Monks (*speaking*)	Yeah Sister!
Crumblitious	She don't fly forwards, no siree,
	She don't fly sidewards, if you please.
	When the Pippitfly flies,
	She flies by eating cheese.
Monks	*Hallelujah!*

Harry	Now ol' Crumblitious
	Took his Window Box hoe,
All (*speaking*)	Yeah Sister!
Harry	And ol' Crumblitious hoed,
	And then he sowed.
All (*speaking*)	Yeah Sister!
Harry	And out of that sowed that Crumbly hoed,
	The green green cheese of Pippit growed,
	And tastier cheese
	Was never, ever knowed.
All	*Hallelujah!*
Monks	Now the Pippitfly came
	One day and ate some cheese,
All (*speaking*)	Yeah Sister!
Monks	And I'll be blowed if
	The Pippitfly didn't sneeze!
All (*speaking*)	Yeah Sister!
Monks	And 'cos of that sneeze from the green green cheese
	That growed from the sowed that Crumbly hoed,
	The Pippitfly
	Flies *back*wards, if you please!
All	*Amen!*
Pippitfly (*speaking*)	Ah-chew!
All (*speaking*)	Yeah Sister!
	Yeah Sister!
(*Singing*)	Hallelujah!
(*Speaking*)	Yeah Sister!
	Yeah Sister!
(*Singing*)	Amen!

The Lights fade to a spot on Harry

The Children, Pippitfly, Monks and Crumblitious exit. During the scene change, the Trash Trump and Litter Bugs enter and take their positions

No. 9a Scene Change Music (optional)

Harry Hey! Now where is that Pippitfly taking them? Looks like they are flying past Trash Trump Dump! I ain't never seen a Trash Trump, but I heard stories about 'em since I was just a kid. You know how you just throw stuff away, and never think about what happens to it? Well, rumour has it that these Trumps are made up entirely of litter. Old boots, tin cans … all heaped up into one big pile of Trash Trump. And every piece of litter's got a life of its own too. Litter Bugs, we call 'em. Ever been bitten by an old boot? It ain't nice, I can tell ya. Now can you imagine, if everybody put all their rubbish into one big pile, just how big that pile of rubbish would be? Why, I bet ya it'd be bigger than the whole of China! I sure hope those kids don't stop there!

Lighting change

The children and the Pippitfly enter

They look around curiously at the big pile of rubbish (which can be formed by the Litter Bugs). The Trash Trump is hiding amongst the Litter Bugs

Jesse Why has she stopped at this old dump?
Teddy Jesse, she's a *fly* …
Jesse I know that, Teddy. I'm not stupid.
Teddy I was only saying …

The pile of "rubbish" rustles

Meggie Umm, I don't want to worry anyone, but you see that big pile of rubbish over there?
Jesse Of course we can see it, Meg.
Meggie Well, watch it carefully, because I think it just moved.

The Trash Trump turns to the children, marches over to them, and salutes

Trash Trump Sergeant Trump at your service, ma'am. What can I do for you?
Jesse Oh … umm … Thank you very much, but we're just stopping here on our way to Edgy Forest. We really won't be long, and we don't want to be any bother …
Trash Trump Did you say Edgy Forest? You want to be careful in there, ma'am. That's the home of the Gump Grump.

No. 9b Gump Grump (sting)

Meggie We know that, Sergeant. That's why we're going there. To get back the Sandman's sleeping sand.
Teddy He stole it, you see, but we've got a present to give him so that he'll give it back to us.
Trash Trump A present? You'll need more than that if you are going to see the Gump Grump.

No. 9c Gump Grump (sting)

Better let me give you some weapons, my friends … just in case.

Jesse Weapons? What weapons?
Trash Trump Rubbish …
Meggie What?
Trash Trump Rubbish!
Jesse Well! Excuse me! How rude!
Trash Trump Litter Bugs … Fall in! Atten-shun!

*Lighting change. As the weapons and armour are mentioned in the following
song, they are taken from the rubbish and given to Jessie, Meggie and Teddy*

No. 10 The Trash Trump Dump

Trash Trump	If it's broken, bent or bust
Litter Bugs	If it's broken, bent or bust
Trash Trump	If it's turning into dust
Litter Bugs	If it's turning into dust
Trash Trump	If the smell would make you choke,
Litter Bugs	If the smell would make you choke
Trash Trump	If it's bust or bent or broke
Litter Bugs	If it's bust or bent or broke
Trash Trump (*speaking*)	It's Rubbish!
Litter Bugs (*speaking*)	Rubbish!
Trash Trump (*speaking*)	I said Rubbish!
Litter Bugs (*speaking*)	Rubbish!
Both (*speaking*)	R.U.B.B.I.
	U.B.B.I.S.H.
	R.U.B.B.I.S.H. Rubbish!
Trash Trump	Please specify what you require and we'll do our best, yes sir
Litter Bugs (*speaking*)	Sir yes sir!
Trash Trump	Identify your needs and I will see if they concur …
Litter Bugs (*speaking*)	Concur!
Trash Trump	… With our catalogue, marked A to Zee.
	I've logged each item person'lly,
	And what you get is what you see
All	Here at the Trash Trump Dump.
Litter Bugs	Dump dump
	Dump dump dump dump.
	Dump dump
	Dump dump dump dump.

During this, the children root around in the rubbish

Trash Trump (*singing*)	Now stop right there!
	I've just the thing to give you for protection
Litter Bugs (*speaking*)	Protection!
Trash Trump	I saved some Purple Myrtle Shells
	On the day of their rejection
Litter Bugs (*speaking*)	Rejection!
Trash Trump	An old boot-lace or two will do
	To tie them to the front of you.
	And a little advertising too:
All	Found by the Trash Trump Dump.
Litter Bugs	Dump dump
	Dump dump dump dump.
	Dump dump
	Dump dump dump dump.
Trash Trump	Now depending on your tactics,
	Swords are best for this affray.
Litter Bugs (*speaking*)	Affray!
Trash Trump	But no-one with a sword would want
	To throw the thing away.
Litter Bugs (*speaking*)	Away!
Trash Trump	A Slinging Shot with Stinging Stones,
	A Battleaxe of Boiled Bones,
	And my old Grandma's Solid Scones,
	Cooked at the Trash Trump Dump.
Litter Bugs	Dump dump
	Dump dump dump dump.
	Dump dump
	Dump dump dump dump.
Trash Trump	Well, now my friends, you're certified
	To fight the worst of foes.
Litter Bugs (*speaking*)	Of foes!
Trash Trump	You're tactical and practical
	From your head down to your toes.
Litter Bugs (*speaking*)	Your toes!
Trash Trump (*speaking*)	And when the enemy hears the sound
	Of your victory echoing around,
	Please (*singing*) mention that your gear was found
All	Down at the Trash Trump …
	DU—MP!
Litter Bugs	R.U.B.B.I. B.I.S.H.
All	Rubbish!

By the end of the number, the children are fully armoured and weaponed, and ready for battle. The Lights fade to a spot on Harry

Everyone, except Harry, exits. During the scene change, the Gump Grump enters and hides behind a tree

No. 10a Exit Music, Underscoring and Entrance of Gump Grump

Harry Hey now, there ain't no cause to be happy! You ain't seen nothin' yet. Take it easy going into Edgy Forest. There's some real ugly mothers livin' in there, and the fathers ain't so pretty neither. There's Night Gnats that'll eat you alive if you let 'em, and there's no tellin' what the Gump Grump is like. Oh, I hope those kids can get my sand back. Look out! What's that in the shadows? I can't look! I can't look! (*He hides his face in his hat*)

Lighting change

The children enter cautiously into Edgy Forest. Suddenly, a huge shadow appears and loud footsteps echo around them. The children stand staring at the shadow, frozen with fear

Jesse (*whispering*) Get the present ready!
Meggie (*whispering*) Never mind the present! Get the weapons ready!

The girls nervously hold up their weapons as Teddy decides to go and have a look behind the tree from which the noise is emanating

Jesse (*whispering*) Teddy! What are you doing?

During the musical crescendo, he walks up to the tree and peeks behind it cautiously

Teddy grabs hold of the Gump Grump and yanks him out from behind the tree. The Gump Grump is holding a bag with "SAND" written on it

Teddy Guys, it's OK. He's only little, look.
Jesse I *told* you we should have gone with the present!
Meggie Are *you* the Gump Grump?
Gump Grump Of course I am! What do I look like to you, a Snoodle Werp? Pah. Leave me alone. Go away or I'll set the Crovel on you.
Meggie But he's only little!
Teddy I know how he feels …
Jesse (*offering the present*) We've come to get the sleeping sand back, and in return, we bring you this gift of itching powder!

Meggie So if you could just give us the sand, then we'll leave you alone.
Teddy Thank you.
Meggie Oh yes, thank you.
Gump Grump Itching powder? I don't want itching powder! Go away!
Teddy I *knew* that witch was bad news … didn't I say … ?
Jesse Teddy. Shut up. Right. That does it. Troops!
Meg } (*together*) What?
Teddy
Jesse You!
Meg } (*together*) Oh!
Teddy
Jesse Take Up Your Weapons!

They aim their weapons at the Gump Grump

Jesse Now then, the sand, if you please.
Gump Grump Never!

   Suddenly, Jewels the Witch enters, followed by her Henchmen and some Hagglets and Habituals. She looks furious

Children Uh-oh.
Jewels You were supposed to *throw* that at him! (*A sigh*) Give them something simple to do, and they mess it up …
Gump Grump What are *you* doing here, you horrible old witch?
Jewels I have come for the sand! Give me that bag, you vile creature!!

She grabs for the bag. They struggle over it

Meggie What are we going to do now?
Jesse I don't know!
Teddy Quick! The itching powder! Throw the itching powder!
Jewels No! No! Not at me, you fools!

Jesse throws the contents of the present at the Gump Grump and Jewels. There is a pause as they register shock, and then nothing happens

  I'm not itching! Give me that!

Jewels grabs the bottle from Jesse and looks at the bottom of it

  Drat! The first successful spell I have ever made, and the blasted thing has a shelf-life.

Jesse Got any other bright ideas, Teddy?
Teddy Um … we could always … *run*!

Suddenly, as if on cue, the following enter behind the children: the Groogly Hog, the Snoodle Barker, Crumblitious and the Pippitfly, the Trash Trump and a handful of Litter Bugs. Now the sides are pretty evenly matched for number

Trash Trump Never fear! The cavalry's here!
Gump Grump You'll never get the sand! Never!
Trash Trump Company … Take aim!
Jewels I've been waiting for some excitement all day. Let's get 'em!

No. 11 The Final Conflict (instrumental underscore)

Lighting change. A fight ensues, the like of which has not been seen for many years. Jesse and Meggie fight bravely against Jewels, who throws spells at them

All Pow! Biff! Ow! Splat! Wham! Bam!
Jewels I'll get you, my pretties! And your little brother too!

Teddy takes on the Gump Grump single-handedly, but he tries a different tactic

Teddy (*offering a scone*) Here, little fella, have a scone. You know, I've always had trouble being small. How about you?

The Gump Grump nearly falls for it, until Teddy goes for the bag of sand

Now give me the sand, you Gumpy Grumpy Gump!
Gump Grump Never! Never! Get off! Get off!

The Train driver and the Barker pounce on some Habituals

Barker Roll up! Roll up! Come and get defeated, you 'orrible little things!
Train Driver All aboard! All aboard! Enemy this way!

Crumblitious singles out the Henchmen and manages to trip them over his walking stick

Crumblitious Come back, you nasty little … thing, you!

The Pippitfly buzzes around a Hagglet

Hagglet I'll get you, I'll get you, you evil insect of the night! Hey, you've got no wings! How do you fly?

The Litter Bugs handle a group of Hagglets

Litter Bugs Right formation, left wheel, stand at the ready, arm the archers, battle stations, left, right, left, right!

In the midst of all this, everyone begins to notice that Teddy and the Gump Grump are downstage C, tugging at the bag between them. Slowly, everyone else joins their respective side until a huge Tug o' War ensues over the bag

Good Guys Heave!
Bad Guys Ho!
Good Guys Heave!
Bad Guys Ho!
Good Guys Heave!
Bad Guys Ho!
Good Guys Heave!
Bad Guys Ho!
Good Guys Heave!
Bad Guys Ho!
Good Guys Heave!
Bad Guys Ho!

Suddenly, as the music climaxes, the bag splits in two, and the sand (silver and gold glitter) shoots everywhere, landing on everyone's head. There is an almighty shout at this, followed by the usual falling over at the end of a Tug o' War. There is a moment of calm while they all assess the situation

Gump Grump Hey! My bag of sand, You broke it, you horrible little boy! You're gonna have to pay for that! You're going to ... (*yawn*) ... pay ... (*yawn*) ... for ... (*yawn*) ... zzzzz.
Jewels Wake up ! Wake up, you Grump! You stupid ... (*yawn*) ... silly ... (*yawn*) ... little ... (*yawn*) ... zzzzz.
Creatures I'm so tired! Me too ... I think I'll have a little kip now ... Gosh, fighting can make you tired, can't it? (*etc., etc.*)

One by one, all of the creatures begin to nod off, until the children are the only ones left awake

Jesse Oh no ... (*yawn*) ... look at the sand ... it's everywhere ... (*yawn*) now we'll never get it back to Harry ... zzzzz.

Meggie We've failed … (*yawn*) … no-one will ever sleep again … (*yawn*) … what are we going to do … zzzzz.

Teddy That's all very well (*yawn*) but how are we (*yawn*) supposed to get … home …now … zzzzz.

The children et al. *are fast asleep. The Lights fade to a spot on Harry, who has taken off his hat, and is catching the falling sand in it. He gestures his arm across to where the children are asleep*

Everyone, except Harry, exits. During the following song, the scene is changed back to the bedroom where the children are asleep in bed

No. 12 The Sandman's Lullaby

Harry (*speaking*) Close your eyes as the chime of the time
                           Sends a rhythm through your mind
                           That beats softly, softly … Hush now …
                           Take your soul for a stroll down the Boulevard of Dreams.
                           Let the beat of your feet on the street kick up a little dust
                           Into the atmosphere. Here,
                           Where your wishes dare to mingle with the crowd,
                           Humming the blues ain't allowed.
                           Reach …
                           Into your pocket,
                           Pull out a handful of fears,
                           A palmful of tears and then blow
                           (Whooo). Watch them go as you ease on through
                           A dream or two …
                           As you ease on through
                           A dream or two …

Harry creeps over to the bed where the children are curled up, fast asleep. Lighting change. He sits on the edge of the bed and clicks his fingers over them. The girls wake up slowly, but Teddy sits bolt upright in bed, punching the air

Teddy (*shouting*) I'll get you, you Gumpy Grumpy Gump Grump you! Give me that sand! Hey, Jesse, Meg! Wake up! We're home! We're home!

Jesse Oh Harry, we really *tried* to get back the sand ——

Meggie — but it all went everywhere when the bag broke, and ——

Jesse — and we're really sorry … and ——

Harry Hey! Tell me something … did you guys have a good sleep?

Teddy I had a lovely sleep … and I dreamt about Snoodle Werps, and Oozeberry Pie, and Trash Trumps, and all *sorts* of things …

Harry You dreamt about *what*? Boy, you sure do have some crazy dreams. Well, that must have been due to this here hatful of sand I got …
Jesse The sand!
Meggie You've got it!
Jesse Which means there is nothing else to do, right Harry?
Harry (*pouring the sand from his hat into a pocket, and putting his hat on again*) Just one thing to do, little lady …

No. 13 Finale (Reprise: Gospel Prayer)

(*To the band*) Hit it!

All the other kids come running on as the children's friends again

Chorus (*singing*)	Well your task is done and you did just fine.
Harry	Do you hear that melody divine?
Chorus (*speaking*)	We wanna dance, we wanna sing.
Harry	Now I've got the chance to do my thing.
Chorus (*singing*)	That Sand will brush across the land
Harry	And bring you sleep at my command.
Chorus (*speaking*)	So spread the Sand out at the double
Harry	'Cos there ain't gonna be no more big trouble.
Chorus (*singing*)	Oo-oo, no more big trouble.
	Oo-oo, no more big trouble.
	Oo, no trouble.
	Oo, no trouble.
Jesse	We fought the fight and we faced the foe.
Meggie	And now there ain't no worries any more!
Teddy	'Cos we are here to help you!
Chorus	Help him!
Teddy (*speaking*)	Help you …
Chorus (*singing*)	Help him!
Teddy (*speaking*)	Help you …
Chorus (*singing*)	Help him!
Teddy (*speaking*)	Help you …
Chorus (*singing*)	Help him!
Teddy (*speaking*)	Help you …
Chorus (*singing*)	Help him!
Teddy (*speaking*)	Help you …
Chorus (*singing*)	Help him!

Teddy (*speaking*) *Stop!*

Harry (*speaking*)   You helped me (*singing*) find the Sand, yeh yeh yeh
                                   yeh, yeh
                               So I can spread my glorious sleep all over the land.

Chorus   Yeh yeh yeh yeh

Harry }
Chorus }   Amen!

Harry (*speaking to the audience*)
                               So how about it? Are you guys gonna help us finish the
                               show?

All (*singing*)   Oh, yeah!

No. 13a Bows

No. 13b Encore (Reprise: The Bed Bug Bop)

All   We've got the Bed Bug Bop (We've got the Bed Bug Bop)
We've got the Bed Bug Bop (We've got the Bed Bug Bop)
We've got the Bed Bug Bop (We've got the Bed Bug Bop)
We've got the Bed Bug Bop
We've got the Bed Bug Bop, the Bed Bug Bop
We're hopping and bopping and we just can't stop
We've got the Bed Bug Bop, We've got the Bed Bug Bop
We're hopping, bopping,
Jiving and diving,
Mopping, popping,
Hiving and thriving.
We're scooting, squealing,
Hooting and reeling,
Peaking, poking,
Squeaking and joking.
We're swaying, playing,
Feeling in the pink.
Don't think we'll ever stop
With the Bed Bug, with the Bed Bug,
With the Bed Bug, with the Bed Bug Bop.
With the Bed Bug Bop!
YEAH!

No. 13c Exit Music

CURTAIN

FURNITURE AND PROPERTY LIST

On stage: Rostra. *Hanging above upstage edge*: window frame
Moon and stars mobile
Map of the journey, with symbol of Jesse, Meggie and Teddy on a pin, hanging UL
Toy box. *In it*: toy train; 3 small flags (lilac, lemon yellow, candyfloss pink); large, black spell book; clear jar with bright green toad and 2 string mice-tails; large, blue, glass goblet containing talcum powder; 2 pairs of maracas (one pair peppermint green, one pair lilac). *On it*: toy carousel
Alphabet blocks

To open: Powder blue chintz bedspread, 3 small pillows with lemon yellow pillowcases set on rostra for bed

Off stage L: Large train engine (with smoke machine pre-heated inside boiler section)
Candyfloss pink baby Snoodle Werp hand-puppet (**Snoodle Barker**)
Bright pink, blue, green and yellow children's umbrellas (**Chorus**)
Lilac cotton pear on sticks, in a wicker basket (**Daisytattle(s)**)
Powder blue chintz river for Window Sill falls
Punnets: powder blue, lilac and candyfloss pink selection, with contrasting ribbons (**Monks**)
3 lilac "Purple Myrtle shells" with black "TTD" and lilac twine neck-loops (**Litter Bugs**)
Scone bag (candyfloss pink chintz with lemon yellow writing "Scones") (**Litter Bugs**)

Off stage R: Buckets of silver glitter (**Clowns**)
3 candyfloss pink Snoodle Werps for **Jessie, Meggie** and **Teddy**
Cauldron for **Jewels**
2 peppermint green leaf and lilac trunk trees (short tree: candyfloss pink and lilac oozeberry pies; tall tree: lemon yellow doughnuts and powder blue Spiky So-So Nuts)
Hessian seed bag on twine, Pippit Cheese hessian bag, walking stick (**Crumblitious**)
2 small wicker baskets (**Villagers**)
Reversible sign ("Trash Trump Dump" and "Edgy Forest")
Slinging shot: powder blue with white string, not practical (**Litter Bugs**)

Battleaxe of Boiled Bones: peppermint green blade, lemon yellow handle (**Litter Bugs**)

Hessian sandbag with powder blue writing "SAND" (velcro'd together down both edges), containing silver and gold glitter (**Gump Grump**)

COSTUME PLOT

Basic costume
Jesse
    Candyfloss pink T-shirt with lemon yellow moon and stars logo outlined in black
    Blue denim shorts
    Candyfloss pink bed-hat
Meggie
    Lilac T-shirt with lemon yellow moon and stars logo outlined in black
    Blue denim shorts
    Lilac bed-hat
Teddy
    Lemon yellow T-shirt with lemon yellow moon and stars logo outlined in black
    Blue denim shorts
    Lemon yellow bed-hat
Ensemble
    Powder blue T-shirt with lemon yellow moon and stars logo outlined in black
    Blue denim shorts

(All with bare feet)

Harry
    White T-shirt
    Off-white cricket trousers
    Black belt
    Silver glitter tail-coat with deep blue lining
    Powder blue pocket handkerchief
    Off-white fedora hat with powder blue hatband
    Deep blue and white baseball boots
Jewels
    Calf-length close-fitting evening gown with elaborate gold trimming and low V
        neck
    Long, black, satin evening gloves
    Sheer black stockings
    High-heeled black shoes
    Copious amounts of diamante jewellery

Additions to basic costume to indicate creature

Henchmen:
The short one
    Very large scruffy black tail-coat
    Very large scruffy old top-hat

Peppermint green pocket handkerchief
Scruffy black Doc Marten boots
Black bow-tie

The tall one
Very small scruffy black tail-coat
Very small scruffy old top-hat
Peppermint green pocket handkerchief
Scruffy black Doc Marten boots
Black bow-tie

Off stage R

Gospel Choir
White cotton cassocks with long sleeves and round necks
Hagglets and Habituals
Black fingerless gloves
Black woollen hats
Crumblitious
Sack with hole for head and split down sides, with Peppermint Green fabric patch
    on the front painted with a Candyfloss Pink and Lilac flower, and belt of
    coloured twine tied around waist
Large straw hat with Peppermint Green band
Peppermint Green walking stick
Pippitfly
Lilac skateboarding knee-pads, elbow pads and wrist pads
Lilac antennae (ping-pong balls) on lilac headband
Lilac, white and candyfloss pink ostrich feathers tucked into waistband at the back
    of lilac lycra dance tights
Gump Grump
Peppermint green baseball cap worn backwards with a lilac "GG" above the peak

Off stage L

Groogly Hog
Train driver's peaked cap, powder blue
Clowns
Candyfloss pink curly clown wigs, 1 lilac curly clown wig
Large, candyfloss pink bow-ties, 1 large, lilac bow-tie
Large, bright red nose
Daisytattle
Petal head-dress, front of petals lilac and back peppermint green
Snoodle Barker
Lemon yellow cotton waistcoat
Lemon yellow neckerchief
Black bowler hat with lemon yellow headband

Snoodle Grooms
>One candyfloss pink, one lilac, one peppermint green neckerchief

Scrumble Bees
>Lemon yellow net wings attached by elastic
>Lemon yellow antennae (ping-pong balls) on yellow head-band

Hagglets and Habituals
>Black fingerless gloves
>Black woollen hats

Monks
>Sack with hole for head and split down sides, with Peppermint Green fabric patch on the front painted with a Candyfloss Pink and Lilac flower, and belt of coloured twine tied around waist

Trash Trump
>Powder Blue rubbish bag with hole for head and arms
>Powder Blue American GI helmet with net covering and chin strap
>Powder Blue short cane
>Large black comedy moustache
>All five colours: medals on chest

Litter Bugs
>Powder Blue rubbish bag with hole for head and arms.

LIGHTING PLOT

Property fittings required: nil

To open: House lights at full and open-stage preset

Cue 1	Front of House clearance *House lights and preset out*	(Page 1)
Cue 2	At the beginning of "The Bed Bug Bop" *Slow build to general bright full-stage wash*	(Page 1)
Cue 3	At the end of "The Bed Bug Bop" *Slow cross-fade to shadowy, night-time wash*	(Page 3)
Cue 4	**Harry** snaps his fingers *Snap to heavenly light for* **Gospel Choir**	(Page 6)
Cue 5	**Harry** rolls the toy train off stage *Cross-fade to general, bright, full-stage wash (fairground)*	(Page 11)
Cue 6	**Jesse**: "Let's fly over that!" *Cross-fade to spot on* **Harry**	(Page 13)
Cue 7	**Harry**: " ... tell her about the Gump Grump ..." *Cross-fade to shafts of light through a gloomy atmosphere*	(Page 13)
Cue 8	**Jewels** casts a spell at the children overhead *Lightning*	(Page 14)
Cue 9	**Jewels** trills a calypso arriba *Snap to sunny Caribbean general full-stage wash*	(Page 19)
Cue 10	**Jewels**: "Fools, everywhere ..." *Cross-fade to spot on* **Harry**	(Page 22)
Cue 11	**Harry**: "Let's see where they got to ..." *Slow cross-fade to blue wash over Window Sill Falls*	(Page 22)
Cue 12	**Jesse**: "... stop for a minute ..." *Cross-fade to general bright full-stage wash*	(Page 22)

EFFECTS PLOT

Cues 4 and 5 are optional

Cue 1	The children watch the town *Clock strikes midnight*	(Page 3)
Cue 2	Large train enters *Smoke rises from the train's funnel*	(Page 11)
Cue 3	**Jewels** casts a spell *Thunder*	(Page 14)
*Cue 4	Top of musical introduction to "Jewels" *Spider lowered from the flys*	(Page 14)
*Cue 5	**Jewels**: "Fools, everywhere ..." *Spider flown back up to the flys*	(Page 22)
Cue 6	As the children enter Edgy Forest *Loud, echoing footsteps*	(Page 30)
Cue 7	As the bag of sand splits in half *Silver and gold glitter drop over the stage*	(Page 33)